THE GREENEST ISLAND

# PAUL
# THEROUX

## THE GREENEST ISLAND

penguin books

PENGUIN BOOKS
Published by the Penguin Group
Penguin Books USA Inc., 375 Hudson Street,
New York, New York 10014, U.S.A.
Penguin Books Ltd, 27 Wrights Lane,
London W8 5TZ, England
Penguin Books Australia Ltd, Ringwood,
Victoria, Australia
Penguin Books Canada Ltd, 10 Alcorn Avenue,
Toronto, Ontario, Canada M4V 3B2
Penguin Books (N.Z.) Ltd, 182–190 Wairau Road,
Auckland 10, New Zealand

Penguin Books Ltd, Registered Offices:
Harmondsworth, Middlesex, England

Published in Penguin Books 1995

"The Greenest Island" first appeared in the *New Review* and later in Mr.
Theroux's *World's End and Other Stories*, Houghton Mifflin, 1980.

ISBN 0 14 60.0117 6

Printed in the United States of America

# THE GREENEST ISLAND

## 1

They had chosen San Juan because it was cheap that year and it was as far away as they could get from people who knew they were not married. They guessed they would be found out eventually, but to be caught at home, mimicking marriage, playing house—that was dangerous. They were in trouble and ashamed of it, but being young felt the shame as an undeserved insult. They had discovered this island like castaways in a children's story, who stumble ashore and learn to live among the surprises of a tropical place. The footprints of cannibals, bright birds, coconut palms!

But in 1961 Puerto Rico was a poor ruined island. There was no romance—they had brought none. It was green, that was all; and though the green was overstated, there was a kind of yellow delay lurking in the color. They were unprepared and a little frightened. They had nothing but their pretense of audacity and three hundred and twenty dollars. No return tickets: they had no particular plans. The hotel was dirty and expensive—they couldn't live there. By chance, they found a furnished room on the Calle de San Francisco. It was only a room, but here they felt safe enough to write to their families and tell them what they had done.

Paula had hidden her pregnancy from her parents. She had planned to tell them, but for four months she had lived with Duval in his college town—another shabby room. She wrote home then; she told them she was in New York, working. I need a year off, she said. Her parents understood. There were two other couples in that house—newly married students, with stingy interests, busy with their studies, wanting privacy in their nests of notebooks and term papers. Noisy and hilarious in their rooms, outside they were incurious. Duval saw them on the stairs and couldn't match the nighttime laughter to their grave daylit faces. When the spring semester ended, Paula had said, "I can't go home—they'd kill me," and Duval had agreed to do something.

He was nineteen, impatient to be older and with a sense that he was incomplete. He read; his imagination blazed; he tried to write. Although he had accomplished little he had the conviction that he was marked for some great windfall, without sacrifice. He believed in his luck, and this belief made him unassailable but solitary and secretive. He could do whatever he chose to; he was confident of his ability to write humorously and well. His spark warmed him like a star and promised that success would come to him with age, in a matter of years. He was certain of it, but that was before Paula had shrunk this future he imagined. Her news had brought the future to his feet, unexpectedly freezing him. He was no longer alone. She was twenty-one, a woman, and she resented the difference in their ages, though she looked younger than he with her sly pretty face and straight blond-streaked hair and warm skin. He had loved her.

A year before he might have married her. But he had stopped loving her, the fever left him, and a month later she had said he'd made her pregnant. It happened so fast there wasn't time to talk about their feelings, and Duval didn't want to hurt her more by saying he didn't love her. Love didn't matter now. The fact was greater: she was going to have his baby. For a confused month when they were apart, in letters, they had argued about the alternatives. The thought of an abortion frightened her. "Knitting needles," she said. He calmed her and telephoned a woman in Somerville. The woman said she would do it for sixty dollars and that he should call back. He did, a week later. The woman was hysterical; she screamed, she cried. She would be arrested, she said in a terrible voice. But she agreed to do it. "It's the last time!" Duval never called her again. And it was too late to get married, because now they knew what their marriage would be: a temporary urgency, a trap, the end of their lives. They wanted more than that and they knew they were not in love.

Still, they were afraid; but less afraid when they were together. They would stay together and hope and try to be kind. They had no choice. And yet they wished to believe that some miracle would release them, that they would wake up free one morning. The wish made them restless and it convinced them that if Paula weren't pregnant, if there were no child, they would not be together.

It seemed necessary to flee and hide. Their parents had begun to wonder about them. Duval said he was going to work on a ship; Paula wrote that she was spending the summer in New York. And when their parents were satisfied with these explanations they flew to San Juan. It was like a 3 further possibility of hope: such a great distance to such a strange place; the humid heat, the smells, yellow-brown faces, the sight of palms. The miracle might happen here, on this green island. They waited in their room.

In the morning from their window they could see the high stucco houses of the old city with their cliff-like balconies, and the ramparts of the fort and the jutting roofs of the settlement that was pitched between the sea wall and the ocean, the stick and palm leaf slum known locally as *La Perla*, the pearl. There was music, one song played over and over, yakking trumpets, the snap of guitars and sad Spanish tenors. There were cries from the street: the paper seller calling out "—*parcial*," the chattering of the boy beggars, the ice-cream man with his cart of *piraguas*; and the frantic din of an old woman yelling in Spanish. They heard her for days—she sounded hurt—and then, when they saw her, she was doing nothing more alarming than selling lottery tickets in front of the Colorama Toy Store. She had to scream. Her competitor was a dwarf with tiny legs and an enormous head, who sat in a chair in the Plaza Colon, just around the corner. He looked at first glance like a severed head propped on a chair seat, and most people bought their tickets from him, for charity, for luck.

Duval explored the neighborhood and brought back stories. The people were damaged and crazy, or else very sad. There were homeless boys and old women who slept on the marble benches in the plaza, under the statue of Columbus. The paper seller—his face burned black, his hair burned orange—stood in the sun all day, and at night got drunk and wept hoarsely and shook his penis at passers-by. There was a one-legged man who wore a red scarf on his head and when he paused to beg hooked his stump over the bar of his crutch and glared like a pirate and demanded money. There was a legless man who rode up and down the Calle de San Francisco in a low clattering cart, pulling himself along with his hands. One morning Duval saw a group of excited men being harangued by a soldier. "They are starting an army," said an onlooker. "They will invade Santo Domingo and kill Trujillo."

It rained each afternoon, sometimes for a few minutes, occasionally for twenty minutes or more. It was loud; it crackled like burning sticks and drove people into doorways—the crazy ones, the five-dollar whores from La Gloria, the beggars, schoolgirls, amputees, the recruits for the invading army—and there they waited, watching the rain, not speaking. After the rain the buildings dripped and there would be a hot hideous smell in the air of wet garbage and yellow sunlit vapor rising from the street. There were few tourists—it wasn't the season. There were sailors from the navy base and merchant seamen who crowded in from the docks and lingered in the plaza where there were whores and shade and cigar stalls.

It looked dangerous—an island of fugitives, temporary people and harmed hopeless souls. Paula and Duval felt they belonged there: such strangeness could make them anonymous. But they were scared, too—worried they'd be robbed, uncertain about the future, so far. Duval went out alone during the day, and at night, when the old city was those harsh 5 voices and songs and the sound of traffic and the roar of the sea near La Perla, he stayed in with Paula. At midnight all the radios in the district played the national anthem: *La tierra di Borinquén; donde me nacido. Isla de flores*—Duval knew the words, but not their meaning.

Their room faced the street. There were two other rooms on that floor, Mr. Ruiz's and Antonio's. Mr. Ruiz lived in Arecibo. He went home to his family at weekends and on Sunday night returned alone to his room, bringing a bag of mangoes. He said he hated his room. He said, "It can get very bad here." He hated the ants, the cockroaches, the darkness. "I burn the ants," he said, and then, "I like to hear the little snaps when they die."

Antonio disliked Mr. Ruiz; Antonio wanted Puerto Rico to be the fifty-first state, Mr. Ruiz wanted independence. When he saw Paula and Duval, Antonio always called out, "State fifty-one!" Antonio worked at night—he never said where. In the afternoon he stood in the doorway on Calle de San Francisco muttering each time a woman went past: *"Fea . . . fea,"* ugly, ugly. He said he did it to engage them, and sometimes they stopped and talked and went upstairs with him. He lived in the next room and those times his elbows knocked on the wall and his bed creaked as if it were being sawed in half.

The building was owned by Señora Gonzales, a young plump widow who dressed heavily in black. Her curio shop was on the ground floor, and all afternoon she made souvenirs out of coconut fiber and bamboo, place mats and dolls with witches' faces. She was uncritical without being friendly. She had rented Paula and Duval the room and had asked no questions. She had sized them up swiftly and appeared to know they had run away.

They began going out together, always choosing the same route: down to the plaza, over to the fort, up the hill to the cathedral where Ponce de León was buried, and then meeting their own street at the top end, at Baldorioty de Castro. They spoke to no one; the language was incomprehensible. They bought food by pointing and smiling and showing their money: a child's effort, a child's gestures. Each day they had the same meal: mushroom soup thickened with rice, pineapple, ice cream; Paula drank a quart of milk. They kept a record of their expenses and saw their money trickling away. Dreadful; it was what they expected. This green disfigured place was the world. It was hot during the day and at night it stank. There were cripples everywhere. But they had sought it, and they deserved to be here. It matched their own punished mood. And sometimes they felt lucky to be surviving it. No one here could accuse them of betraying their parents. They were what they seemed, a young couple expecting a baby, anonymous in the tropical crowd.

They seldom quarreled. Although they felt they hadn't the right to be happy, they experienced a tentative enjoyment, a little freedom alone in this restricted place. Their occasional anger they made into silence. Paula decided to study Spanish, Duval to write—soon, to use the time.

Alone; but they were not alone. Both sensed it. There was someone else who crouched darkly between them. They dwelled in the present and moved forward only by time's 7 slow fractions. They did not speak of the future because they would not mention the baby. They avoided all talk of that—the choice it demanded, the rush of time it implied. It was more than a weight: it was a human presence. They spent their evenings talking without consequence of the oddities they saw—the religious processions, the green lizards on the back roof, the amputee in his noisy cart: the sunlight removed the cheating blur of nightmarishness and made each sight a vivid spectacle.

They were aware of their omission. It was as if there were a third person with them, sentient but mute, to whom they could not refer without risking misunderstanding or offense. It was someone they did not know, as mysterious to them as anyone on the island, and contained by Paula—when she came close to whisper she bumped Duval with the stranger. And so their evenings had sudden silences and were usually stilled by the sense of a small helpless listener. They were like people sitting in a room to wait for a signal from that third person, and there was about their gentleness a fearful timidity of waiting that was as solemn as a deathwatch.

Others reminded them of why they were waiting. Mr. Ruiz, who gave them mangoes, brought out pictures of his children and named them: Angel, Maria, José, Pablo, Costanza. His wife, he said, was also pregnant: he nudged Duval, trying to share the pride and resignation of fatherhood. Antonio was respectful, and when he saw Duval alone in La Gloria he asked, "How is she?" as if Paula were ill and Duval needed reassurance. Paula remained healthy, though she complained of the humidity and said walking made her feet swell. So each afternoon she lay down and rested. One day, two weeks after their arrival on the island, she said her ankles felt huge. Duval massaged them and said, "Does that hurt?" She said no. He pressed harder; she didn't react. He said, "You're all right," but several minutes later he looked again at the ankle and saw the deep dent of his thumbprint.

The heat drugged them. They went to bed when they heard the national anthem and did not wake until the traffic and street noise racketed against the shutters. She slept soundly, perspiring, a film of heat on her skin; but just before she dropped off to sleep she thought how cruel it all was. Anyone else would have been happy, expectant, making preparations. She was doubtful and afraid. She wanted something else; she was too young to give in to this. A life she did not want was being forced upon her.

Duval's sleep was shallow, disturbed by the last thing he did before he went to bed. This was his journal. Not a diary—he never mentioned the progress of the pregnancy; he wrote undated paragraphs about what he saw on the island. It was, he knew, the sort of book a castaway might keep, a record of wonders and surprises: the beggars, the difficult heat, the ants, the lizards. He did not write about himself. He wanted to survive, and he still believed in his luck. He went to bed; he remembered; he woke up and dreaded to inquire where he was or why. He felt he was performing a service, obediently, unwillingly, without love—as if he had been assigned this protective task for a certain period. When it was over he would be free. But he worried. He had already been away too long; he would not be able completely to re-enter 9 that former self. This task, this place, was undoing him, and he feared that having been forced this far he might never go back.

The silence was broken one night by Paula's crying. He tried to comfort her. He said it was hot—he would open a shutter.

"No," she said. She hadn't moved. She lay on her side, facing away from him. In a small clear voice she said, "What are we going to do?"

2

It was a holiday on the island, Muñoz Rivera's birthday. They had no idea who he was, but the plaza was festive, jammed with buses and taxis and decorated with banners showing Muñoz Rivera's big pink *hidalgo* face. The dark mob, sweating with gaiety, surged beneath the blowing portraits. The shops were closed, there were no newspapers, and even the girls from La Gloria were taking the day off. Duval saw six of them piling into a taxi with towels and baskets of food—off to the beach. Family groups—the scowling fathers walking a little apart—paraded in new clothes up the Calle de San Francisco, on their way to the cathedral.

The activity, the noise, stirred Duval, who was watching it all from the window. He said, "Let's go to the beach."

"How much money do we have?" Paula smoothed her

blouse over her stomach to emphasize the bulge; she was still small.

"Three dollars." But it was less. He knew the exact amount. He hated himself for keeping track.

"The banks are closed today. We'll have to bring sandwiches."

"We don't need money."

She said, "You look like a jack-o'-lantern. I hate your face sometimes."

He looked away. The music outside jumped to the window, the same song; and now he could make out the words, *el pescador* and *corazón*, a mournful blaring, continuously repeated.

She said, "I need a shower."

The shower was in a cement hut on the back roof, where clumsy pigeons sometimes fluttered and nested. Paula took her towel and left, but she returned to the room moments later.

"Cockroaches," she said, and threw down the towel. It was a command.

Duval went to the shower and at first saw none. The room was hot and damp, the toilet stank. A sign next to the toilet was lettered in simple Spanish, DO NOT THROW YOUR PAPER ON THE FLOOR. There was an old obscene picture scratched on the wall, with a one-word caption, *chupo*. A cockroach scuttled across the floor and vanished through a crack—gone before he could step on it. There was movement in the sink. He turned on the faucet and toppled the hurrying thing into the plug-hole and kept the water running to drown it. Then he pushed the plastic shower curtain aside. Two reddish blobs slid scratchily down and began working their legs. Duval pulled off a sandal and slapped at them with the sole; there was one more from the tub, several appeared from behind the sink, and the last climbed from the plug-hole twitching water droplets in its jaws. When he was done Duval had killed nine of them. They were dark and scablike and some flew in an ugly burring way, falling crookedly through the air.

Paula took her shower. Duval gathered the Pepsi-Cola bottles that had accumulated under the bed and returned them at La Gloria for the deposit money. Antonio was there on a stool, hunched over a tumbler of brown rum. Seeing Duval, he spoke.

"You want a nice beach?" Antonio licked at his mustache. "Go to Luquillo."

Duval was mystified; then he remembered the thin wall on which he heard Antonio's elbows. He said, "How do I get there?"

"Take a bus to Rio Piedras, then a *público*." Antonio smiled. "Puerto Rico—you like?"

"It's okay," said Duval.

"Too hot. New York's better," said Antonio. "I was there. *Mira,* I got a kid too, in New York. But I come back here. You can play with the girls, but your mother's forever."

Duval said, "Who is Muñoz Rivera?"

"George Washington," said Antonio. "Have a drink. Luis, *venga!*"

12    "Some other time." Duval gave the empty bottles to the

barman and bought two Pepsis and a greasy *frijole* with the money.

Antonio said, "Everybody in New York knows me. Ask them."

Paula was making the sandwiches when he returned to the room. She had hard boiled three eggs and was chopping them on a plate. The bread was stiff and there were tiny dots of white mold on the crusts. She scraped the bread, then wiped it with watery mayonnaise. She said, "We need a refrigerator."

"Those sandwiches will be all right."

"No," she said. "There are ants in the cheese."

Duval took the small brick of cheese and starting picking them off. Paula looked disgustedly at him. He wrapped the cheese and dropped it into the wastebasket.

"I was going to throw it away."

"You were going to eat it," she said.

He shook his head. But she was right. The insects no longer bothered him. He believed he had overcome his repugnance. The island was crawling with ants, spiders, cockroaches; during the day there were flies, at night mosquitoes. He brushed them aside; there were too many to kill.

Paula said, "I don't want to go to the beach."

"There's nothing else to do."

They had been to the beach nearby, the one across the road from the Carnegie Library. It lay below a sandy cliff and was rocky and strewn with driftwood and lengths of greasy rope. They had been watched the whole time by prowling children in rags from the shacks of La Perla. They decided 13 to take Antonio's advice and go to Luquillo Beach: Luquillo was famous—it appeared on the travel posters.

It was a long trip, by bus and public taxi, taking them past marshland slums on spindly stilts, high thick canefields broken by fields of young spiky pineapples, and, in the distance, hills as blue and solid as volcanoes. They arrived at the beach at noon and were surprised to find it beautiful and nearly empty. There were groups of picnickers and there was a yellow school bus parked on an apron of broken cement, but there were few people swimming and there was no one lying in the sun.

The beach was white, a crescent of glare shimmering beside a gentle wash of surf in a green bay. The beach itself was not wide; it was entirely fringed by slender palms, and the long fronds swayed like heavy green feathers, making the dry rustling of many kites tumbling in a crosswind, a sound that rose to a hectic flap when the wind strengthened and finally stifled it to a moan. Among the palms children were playing hide and seek; they were quick stripes of light as they ran from trunk to trunk, and their laughter carried through the trees.

Duval and Paula walked down the beach until the schoolchildren were tiny and inaudible. They spread out their towels and lay under a palm and watched the green sea mirror wrinkle in the breeze and flash spangles at them.

"Jake!" She snatched his arm. He looked over and saw in the sand, three feet from her, a dead rat. At her second cry it appeared to move, but that was the lizards, four of them, dark green, darting away at her voice and giving the shriveled carcass movement.

"It's horrible," she said. "Let's go somewhere else."

The lizards raised and lowered their tiny dragon heads and flicked out their tongues. They crept back and resumed feeding on the rat. Paula and Duval had remained motionless, and now they could smell it and hear the flies.

"Wait," said Duval. He got up and, putting the lizards to flight, scooped sand over it until there was only a mound where the stinking thing had been. He smiled at Paula. "Now let's eat."

The sandwiches tasted dustily of decay, the *frijole* was clammy and almost inedible, but they ate without a word. They listened to the rustle of the palms and watched the surf running and curling against the beach. They kept silent; they were new; it was unlucky to complain so soon. A complaint was an admission of weakness, a tactless challenge to the other's strength. Secretly, they wished for rescue—to be delivered from this mock marriage and the certainty of the child. And they craved protection. They were waiting for everything to change, and yet nothing had changed. The sky was unbroken, the sun bore down on the sand, there was no ship in the sea.

Paula had stopped worrying aloud, and Duval admired that in her, but still his affection was tinged with resentment. She had tricked him. He said nothing about that. He knew she felt the same. They were matched in anger.

But her stubborn calm was disturbed by occasional fears. The closest was that Duval would simply leave her—too soon; that she would come back to the room and find him gone. It checked her temper, this fear of desertion: she must not upset him. And he could go easily—he was so young. He got up and walked along the beach a little way, and she saw him as a stranger. It surprised her again to see how skinny he was, in his wrinkled shorts and flapping shirt, faded already, and kicking at the sand, then looking up and making a face at the palm: just a boy, an unreliable boy, who had fooled her.

Duval continued to look at the palm. He stood at the base of the trunk and high up the fronds formed the spokes of a perfect green wheel, at the hub of which was a cluster of shining coconuts. A tropical beach; the sun on the sea; coconuts. It was what he expected from the island: the castaway's vision of survival in the tropical trees. The breeze stirred the palm. Duval took a stone and threw it hard. He missed and tried again and this time hit a coconut. He saw the large thing nod on the fiber that held it.

Paula watched him with increasing irritation. He was so happy, mindlessly pitching stones at the tree. What was wrong with him? He was determined to play. She would have allowed it in a man, but a man didn't behave that way, and this mood in Duval made her feel insecure. She wanted him beside her, attentive, reassuring, and she called out, as she might have to a child, "Stop that!"

Duval paused and shrugged and threw another stone.

"Stop!"

He said, "I want that coconut." He wanted the little victory, the prize. He would get the husk open somehow and offer her the sweet water to drink. And they could eat the white flesh; it would taste better than her sandwiches.

The coconut wouldn't come down. He had hit it squarely but the stones bounced off without dislodging it. He took a heavy stick and threw it and hit it again. The coconut moved slightly, but did not fall. He tried shaking the tree; it did no good. It was such a simple thing, but he could not do it. He threw another stick. This one crashed through the fronds and landed near Paula.

She scrambled to her feet and said, "You almost hit me!"

"Sorry."

"I told you to stop," she said. "Now cut it out."

He left it, and he was annoyed when he returned to her and she looked straight ahead, at the sea. He felt she was mocking him, not because he had tried to knock down the coconut but because he had failed to do it.

She wandered down the beach to the water's edge and holding her skirt against her thighs waded in the shallow surf. Duval looked around; in the distance there were children, and two priests in dark cassocks, brown and yellow stripes between the palm trunks. He slipped off his shorts and put on his bathing suit.

"It's beautiful," he said, coming behind her.

"I wish we could enjoy it." She had said that of the explosive sunsets over the cracked Fortaleza; of the cool plaza; of the gaiety at dusk on the Calle de San Francisco. It was her repetition of it that he hated. That was marriage: repetition.

He strode past her and dived into the water, and was buoyed by its brightness and warmth. It took away his irritation. He swam easily down to the sunlit sea floor, yellow, then blue and green flaked, and he faced depths of purple measured by shafts of light, and flimsy weed stalks trailing up from great smooth boulders. In this colored warmth he experienced a brief sensation of freedom: he was leaving everything behind. He saw his future this way, the happiness he had no words for: success, triumph in a casually chosen place. He moved with weightless ease and it was as if he were breathing underwater, his lungs working without effort. Then a ribbon of cold water passed down his body and he turned and circled back to the hot shallows. He threw his head out of the water, and at the shock of air, the dazzle of bright sun, he gasped.

"You soaked me!" Paula was standing at the shoreline, holding out her sprinkled skirt, exaggerating her distress. "When you dived in you got me all wet. Grow up!"

"It'll dry," he said, and he went close to her.

"Don't drip on me," she said.

"Come in—it's fantastic."

"I don't have a bathing suit." She had tried to find a maternity bathing suit. There were none in the cheap stores: Puerto Rican women didn't swim when they were pregnant. And at the tourists' swim shop at the Hilton they were too expensive.

"You don't need one," he said. "No one's looking." He went into the water again and pulled off his swimming trunks and threw them on the sand.

"No," she said, but she looked around uncertainly. It was 18 the hottest part of the day. The beach was empty, there were no people visible among the trees—the children and the priests had gone; so had the school bus. She was alone and felt tiny and misshapen beside the enormous flat sea. She lifted her skirt, walked a few steps into the water and at once wanted to swim.

She went to the beach, and keeping herself low on the dry sand removed her clothes and folded them, making a neat pile. She entered the water. Instantly, all the heat and heaviness she had felt left her. She had swung out of that clumsy body and into her younger one. She was innocent again. The green sea wrapped her and made her feel small and cool.

They swam apart and spent a long time floating—lying back and letting the sun burn their faces, their ears stopped by the water's hum. Duval swam over and embraced her. She hugged him and he was aroused.

"Stop," she said, feeling him against her. She turned to face the beach. "Not here."

He barely heard her. He slid between her legs, and they crouched, up to their shoulders in the water. His face was hot and he could see a dusting of salt on her cheeks and the sparkle of water drops on the ringlets of hair at her ears. She looked tense, and she bit her lip as he moved inside her. Their shoulders splashed, touched, parted, and splashed again in the swelling water, and they watched each other almost in embarrassment, hearing the gurgle their bodies made. Then he moved rapidly and stiffened and his face went cold. She looked bewildered, on the point of speaking. He kissed her. The water was quite still and near his arm a little strand of scum floated like a lifeless creature from the deep.

After that they gathered their clothes and rested in the shade. Paula was sleeping lightly on her side, pillowing her head on her arm. Duval left her and walked through the palms to where they opened into rough low bush and stocky trees with thin yellow leaves. Beyond this, miles inland, he saw the dense rain forest he had seen from the *público*. It was mountainous, shrouded, blue-black, like a tragic precinct of the island's sunlight. The forest was called El Yunque, and it seemed to him then that those great hanging trees and all those rising mists and shadows were what was in store for him if he gave up. His life would be like that. The forest was blind. He would be lost among the high vines, trapped in their tangle, just another anonymous soul in an immensity of tall trees. The forest warned him as the sea had given him hope, but the forest's threat was worse than any he had known, of a kind of cowering adulthood, promising darkness, the scavenging of naked families. Alone, he could escape it; that forest was the fate of men who were afraid and hid. He was too young to enter it now; it was too early for him to explore such towering shadows, and to be lost now was to be lost forever.

It was after five by the time they left the beach, and they had to wait for a bus in Rio Piedras. When they got back to the old part of the city the lights were on in the plaza and there was about the whole district that atmosphere of exhaustion that follows a festival.

20    The milk had gone sour. Duval bought a pint from La

Gloria and a ham sandwich from a street seller. Paula made a meal of them, then lay on the bed and fell asleep at once, still in her clothes. Duval covered her with a sheet and turned off the lamp. He never felt anything but tenderness for her when he saw her asleep, and he thought if he moved her even slightly she would break.

By the window, in the light from the Colorama Toy Store, he wrote what he had seen that day: the canefields, the green sea, the coconut, the lizards feeding on the rat, and the vast gloomy rain forest. The writing made him hungry; he went downstairs. But in La Gloria he reached for his money and remembered he hadn't gone to the bank. He looked for Antonio—he could have that drink he had promised and borrow some money for a *frijole*. Antonio wasn't there, and seeing all the noisy people in the bar Duval pitied himself.

He considered going for a walk: more hunger, and the sight of the rich eating in the windows of the expensive restaurants further up the Calle de San Francisco. The thought of walking bothered him for another reason: if you had no money you stayed put. He was angry—with himself, with Paula; his anger turned to fear, and the green island became again in those seconds of reproach a dangerous alien place of destination and ruin, an intolerable trap.

In the room he looked at the pages he had written. He read a sentence: it was foolish, about the beach, an expression of pleasure. He tore out the page and crumpled it and he was about to throw it into the wastebasket when he saw the cheese.

He unwrapped it, glancing furtively at Paula. A few ants

still clung to it. It was softened by the heat, and it had sweated, but it did not smell rancid. He knelt on the floor, in the darkness, and nibbled it until it was gone.

## 3

Tame spiders dancing on violin strings; a whiff of ice in the air; rest—wakefulness bleeding from his fingers. The images came to him at the concert; he wrote them down and admired his work. His writing calmed him like music; the concerts helped him think.

They were held every Sunday afternoon at the cultural center, a pretty house surrounded by palms on the Avenida Rivera. The people in the audience were unlikely islanders, pale Spaniards, studious blacks in neat suits, and old frail women in summer dresses. The chamber music was a soothing voiceless encouragement to thought, and the room where the concerts were given was clean and air-conditioned. Paula and Duval sat contentedly in the soft chairs breathing Mozart and cool air. It became one of their activities, like the evening walk to the cathedral or the stroll to the fort to watch the sun drop into the ocean. It was free.

In the confidential way they spoke about themselves they began hesitantly to discuss money and to worry. They had spent about a hundred dollars in a month, but even at this 22 frugal rate—there were no more economies they could make—they knew they would have nothing left in two months. The Sunday concert was free; it cost nothing to walk—but there was food to buy, rent to pay. They said nothing about their return tickets. The knowledge of this little money was a slow ache, a dull physical pain like a smudge of guilt, and the passing days only made it keener.

"I'll have to get a job," said Duval.

"I wish I could help." Paula was bigger now; she shifted her stomach each time she moved, and she tired easily. But still she spoke of wanting to go to Rio Piedras and study Spanish. She had inquired. The course cost twenty-five dollars. They both knew it was out of the question. Her Spanish, his writing: they had come to seem like broken promises. Whatever he wrote looked incomplete, and though they contained striking islands of green imagery, they were fragments, they were linked to nothing.

Paula said, "You could go to the Hilton."

Duval resisted. The Hilton, a mile away, reminded him of what he hated and feared, everything he had left behind; humiliation.

He said he would look for a job, and thereafter, in the mornings, he put on his tie and his limp green suit and set off. Paula wished him luck and seeing her at the head of the stairs he felt sorry for her and pity for himself; he was too young for this—another future was his, not a repetition of this. As soon as he walked into the plaza he lost his will to look. He was hot, he felt tired even before he boarded the city bus. He had no practical skills, he could not speak Spanish. But worse, in the course of those days looking for a job 23 he realized he was spending far more than if he had stayed home: bus fares, lunch, *piraguas*, newspapers. He bought the *Island Times*, the English language weekly, and looked through the classified ads. Secretary, draftsman, chemist, clerk, accountant: there was no job he could do.

But he could write. More and more in this unusual place he felt the knowledge growing in him of an impulse to write, of linking the fragments he had already set down. He could write the sad story he had already begun to live. It was the effect of the green island: surviving here proved his imagination was nimble. To choose solitude again was to become a writer, a heartless choice, rejecting a child to claim freedom.

Without telling Paula he made notes on the concert at the cultural center the next Sunday, and that night he wrote two pages about it. He described the musicians, the palms at the window, the items on the program——he compared it to a menu for a great meal. Rereading it he saw that it was stiffly enthusiastic, full of compliments and meaningless hyperbole, uncritical; yet it was printable. He had worked hard on it. He wondered if he had worked too hard. The light had been bad in the room. He had waited for Paula to sleep before he dared to begin, and twice there were sounds from Antonio's room which stopped him.

In the morning, saying that he was going to look for a job, he went to the offices of the *Island Times* and asked to see the editor. The man had his long legs on his desk, his big feet on the blotter. He had a thick black mustache and only nodded when Duval explained what he had written. He passed the

pages to the man. Keeping his feet up the man read the article. Duval saw in this posture a lack of interest; he watched for a reaction and he thought he saw the man smile.

Duval said, "Can you use it?"

The man said—and Duval realized when he spoke that they were the man's first words—"We'll see."

Then Duval was embarrassed; he felt defeated and wanted to leave. In the street again he remembered that he had not mentioned money.

That Thursday he bought the *Island Times*. His piece was not in it. The news was of the filming of *Lord of the Flies* on Vieques Island, a few miles offshore. There was no mention of the concert.

He went to the Hilton. But it was not as he had imagined it, American and intimidating. The stucco was discolored by the sea air, touched by pale florets of decay; and the Puerto Rican smells of sickly fruit and *frijoles* had penetrated to the lobby. The desk clerk directed him to the personnel office, where in a waiting room there were about ten Puerto Ricans, young men and middle-aged women, who looked as if they had been there all morning. A woman at a table was speaking in Spanish to a nervous man with tough Indian features.

Duval took a seat and waited to be called forward.

"Did you see the ad too?" The man next to him was grinning. He wore a baggy linen suit and a string tie. In his southern accent was the lisp of a Spanish speaker. He had a bald wrinkled head and could have been seventy.

Duval said, "No."

"I knew you was a gringo," said the man. His mustache 25

moved when he grinned. "The ad for their new restaurant—
you ain't seen it? They looking for hands."

"What sort?"

"All kinds—in the kitchen, waiters, pearl divers, people up
front to say, 'Your table is all ready, señor.' All kinds. But not
the doorman. That job's as good as filled. By me."

"So they haven't hired you yet."

"No. But they sure will when they sets eyes on me." The
old man tapped Duval on the shoulder and cackled. "I'se a
*technician* doorman."

The woman at the desk gave Duval an application. He
filled it out and in doing so invented a new man, one who
was twenty-three, who had worked in several restaurants and
lived in San Juan for nearly a year; married.

"Help me with this, will you, old chappie?" said the man
in a whisper. "This here writing's too damned small for my
eyes."

The old man—his name was Ramón Kelly—was illiterate.
Duval read the application and Kelly told him what to write:
born in Louisiana in 1903, a graduate of Shreveport High
School; previous jobs on ships, the *Queen Mary*, the *Huey
Long*, the *Andrea Doria;* married, three children. Kelly antic-
ipated the questions, but Duval could see that Kelly was lying too, inventing a man on the job application.

"Where do I put my John Henry?"

Duval showed him.

Kelly licked the tip of the ballpoint, then touched the line
and made several loops that looked convincingly like a signa-
ture. But the name was not Kelly.

The woman at the desk read Duval's application and gave him a slip of paper. She said, "Go to the restaurant—outside the building and turn left. Report to Mister Boder."

Duval did as he was told, and when he entered the restaurant, with its empty tables and smells of floor wax and fresh varnish and workmen carrying potted palms, he heard a voice say, "We got a live one." Then the man appeared and said loudly, "I hope to God you speak English!"

Over coffee, Mr. Boder said that the restaurant, which was to open in two days, was called The Beachcomber. It was part of a chain of American restaurants specializing in Polynesian food. Mr. Boder was general manager of the Los Angeles Beachcomber and had been sent to San Juan to hire waiters and supervise the opening. He was a bluff perspiring man of about fifty with capped teeth which, although perfectly shaped, were yellow from the cigars he chewed. He was friendly, he called Duval "a fellow sufferer," stuck like himself on this island of unreliable people.

Duval said, "It's a dictatorship."

"I'm glad you told me that." Mr. Boder removed his cigar from his mouth and spat into a wastebasket.

"That's what people say."

"I don't speak Spanish." He said that for a few days he had gone to bed with a copy of *L'Imparcial* and a Spanish-English dictionary, but he had abandoned the effort. He hated the island. He was newly married and missed his wife. "My second wife," he said. "She's about your age, and she's starting to whine. You married?"

"Yes."

27

"So I don't have to tell you," said Mr. Boder. "Ever work in a restaurant?"

Duval said he had.

Mr. Boder seemed disappointed. He said, "I hate the food business. The hours, the complaints. The kitchen's always a madhouse. It's ruined my health." He coughed disgustedly, then said, "Of all the rackets you can get in, the food business is the worst."

A Chinese-looking man came out of the kitchen. He was fat-faced and his black suit matched his scowl. He said, "There's another one in the kitchen. Show them around."

When he had gone, Duval said, "Is he Polynesian?"

"Chinese," said Mr. Boder. "It's all Chinese here. Sure, the decor is Polynesian"—he indicated an outrigger canoe which was suspended from the ceiling of woven grass—"but the food's Chinese and all the cooks are slants. That was Jimmy Lee. Did he look worried to you?"

"No," said Duval.

"He's worried. The Beachcomber himself is coming tomorrow. He's always around for the openings."

A young man came out of the kitchen. He was neatly dressed and looked like the sort of person Duval had seen at the cultural center. He said hello to Mr. Boder.

"Speak English?" said Mr. Boder.

"Yes."

"Just asking. You never know with Puerto Ricans."

"I am Cuban."

"Okay, Castro," said Mr. Boder. "That makes two. You're going to be up front with me, boys. Come over here."

Mr. Boder led them through the restaurant to the bar, which was designed to look like a bamboo and wickerwork hut in the South Seas. He said, "I'm going to tell you one or two things and I want you to remember them, because the Beachcomber's very particular. First, we don't let anyone in here that we wouldn't have in our own homes—company policy. No single broads, no hookers, and no drunks. Never recognize anyone, even if you know his name. Why? Because the woman he's with might not be his wife and maybe he told her his name's Smith. You say, 'Evening, Mister Jones,' and he's screwed. Better not to use any names at all—that's how you get tips. A little discretion. If the joint's full, steer them over here into the bar, and if you have to buy them a drink to keep them there, buy it, but don't have one yourself. Correction—you can have a Coke."

The Cuban said, "Do we have to share our tips with the waiters?"

"That's up to you," said Mr. Boder. "Now, in front of you are thirty-five, maybe forty, tropical drinks. Shark's Tooth, Jungle Juice, Pago-Pago. Forget the names. If anyone asks you what's in it just say it has rum, fruit juice, and some bitters. Confidentially, they all have the same shit in them, but you don't have to tell the Beachcomber that. You know anything about the food business, Castro?"

"Yes," he said sternly.

"Ever work up front?"

"I worked at the Hilton in Havana."

"I'm supposed to keel over," said Mr. Boder to Duval. He 29

stared at the Cuban. "Know how important the telephone is?"

The Cuban nodded.

Mr. Boder said to Duval, "Pick up that phone and say, 'Good evening, the Beachcomber.'"

Duval lifted the phone. "Good evening, the Beachcomber."

"Say it as if you mean it."

"Good evening, the Beachcomber."

"You sound like a mortician," said Mr. Boder. "Watch me. I'll show you how it's done." He bared his yellow teeth and spoke genially into the phone.

Later that afternoon Mr. Boder said, "You're on duty tomorrow at four o'clock. Press party, so sharpen up. Don't wear that tie. You're meeting the Beachcomber himself."

Duval heard a low whistle as he left the restaurant. He turned and saw a man in a military cap with a braided visor, and more braids and buttons on a green frock coat. The trousers had a yellow stripe and white piping on the seam. It was Kelly. He said, "One cigarette before you go."

Duval shook out a cigarette and handed it over.

"I told you I'd get the job," said Kelly. Then he frowned at the cigarette. "Look at that, old chappie," he said, pinching the filter tip. "Should be tobacco there, but there's only cotton. They think they're smart and we get it! I'm going to tell the queen about that."

Duval lit the cigarette for him and said, "So you're the 30 doorman."

Kelly smiled. "I'se a *technician* doorman. Ain't nothing I don't know about opening doors."

The Beachcomber was a potbellied man with a bullying voice and a wooden leg. At the press party he banged his cane on the carved figures and chair legs as he limped from room to room. His white hair was cut very short, his forearms stained with tattoos, and when he saw Duval he said, "Don't stand there like a goddamned Prussian. Look alive!"

He left the island the next day for a tour of the Caribbean, and then the restaurant got its first customers. There were not many; it was not the season. One of the dining rooms, The Tortuga, remained closed.

At the end of that week Duval brought his pay home. With tips it came to forty-five dollars. Paula enrolled for the Spanish class and they had their first meal in a restaurant, *arroz con pollo* at La Gloria. Duval had wanted to take her to The Beachcomber, but employees were forbidden to eat there; in any case, he doubted whether he could afford it.

The job gave him a routine. He was free for most of the day. If Paula did not have a Spanish class they walked or went to the beach—the narrow, rocky one across from the Carnegie Library. At three, Duval had a shower and then took the bus along the seafront to work. After two weeks of this he felt like a legitimate resident of the island and thought no more of leaving. Now the island which had once seemed to rock in the ocean like a raft looked vast and green. He was aware that he had spent the entire time at its edge, on the shore; the interior he imagined wild, small towns in dusty jungle where people lived ensnared. But he was safe. He had his work.

The work itself was simple. He answered the telephone and took reservations. He met customers at the door and showed them to their tables. He adjusted the volume of the Hawaiian music on the loudspeakers and kept the lights dim. The customers were mainly middle-aged couples on vacation who had come to the island because the summer prices were so low. There were young wary couples who, tanned and uneasy, he took to be honeymooners. There were secretaries, groups of three or four, who lingered over their meals and held conversations with the waiters. Now and then Duval would see a man eating alone, reading a book, and he would want to sit down and talk to the man. But he kept his place. It appalled him to think that he had in such a short time become so old, so obedient.

"The days of the free lunch are over," said Ramón Kelly, one day. "They haven't paid me for three weeks. I'm going to have to give up this nice old job."

"Do you get tips?"

"Chickenfeed," said Kelly. "My second wife lives up in Key West. She's rolling in it. I'm going up there pretty soon, open a Melanesian restaurant. Gonna get two tall Cubans for the door—black ones, these big fellas. And serve Melanesian food." He grinned.

Duval looked at Kelly's feet.

"Them's my Hoover shoes," said the old man.

Mr. Boder told him not to talk to Kelly on duty. Mr. Boder had become irritable. "You're having yourself a holiday," he said to Duval one evening when he found him reading at the telephone stand. But Mr. Boder was servile with customers and Duval noticed that his moments of servility only made him more bad-tempered with the staff, particularly the Cuban, whom he called Castro.

The Cuban resented the name and refused to say what his real name was. "I don't care," he said. "Batista was the one I hated."

"What was the Havana Hilton like?" asked Duval.

"Very nice." The Cuban clicked his tongue. *"Muchachas."*

"Whenever I hear about Havana I think of Hemingway."

"He used to come in now and then. We kept a certain wine for him—a rosé, nothing special. He always got drunk and shouted. He threw food around the table. 'Pass the bread.' He throw the bread. 'Pass the salt.' He throw the salt. Hemingway. People say he is a great writer. But they don't know. I have seen him with these eyes. He is a pig."

"Have you read his books?"

"I would never read the books of such a pig."

One meal was included. The employees ate in shifts before opening time, but not in the restaurant. They ate rice and beans in the hotel cafeteria, and Duval's half-hour always coincided with Kelly's. Kelly seemed to grow crazier. He said he was British and threatened to go back to England. "Back to Piccadilly, old chappie," he said. He complained that he still had not been paid and said he wanted to kill Mr. Boder with a broken bottle. One evening, in the cafeteria, he asked Duval to write a letter for him. Duval said he would.

Kelly instantly pulled a crumpled sheet of paper from the pocket of his green frock coat. He said, "Got a pen?"

Duval took out his pen and smoothed the paper. He said, "Hurry up. I have to go back in a few minutes."

"I knew you'd help me," said Kelly. "Will you write what I say?"

"Of course."

"Ready?" Kelly folded his arms. "Dear President Kennedy—"

"Wait a minute," said Duval.

"Dear President Kennedy," said Kelly in his lisping drawl. "I'm an old man and I'm stuck on this goddamned island of Puerto Rico living with a widow lady. The bastards haven't paid me—you're not writing!"

"I am."

"Show me."

Duval pushed the paper to him, but Kelly lost interest in it as soon as he saw the scribble. Before Duval could begin again, Kelly said, "My old woman run out on me and the widow lady took pity. That was before the Florida business which I aim to tell you about. Bitch said she was going to Santurce and that's the last I hear from her. I couldn't find a ship. I been working on ships since I was so high and I had a right terrible life—goddamned tax people chasing me, I didn't know which way to turn. Mister President, sir, you can help me if you read this here letter—"

Duval had stopped writing. Kelly had begun to cry. In the
cafeteria, in his bandsman's uniform, surrounded by chatter-

ing Puerto Ricans, the old man sat shaking his bald head. He continued to weep. The tears ran into his mustache.

But later that night Duval saw him out front. He was shutting the door of a limousine and saluting to the man who had just stepped inside.

"Boder says you're married," he said when the car drew away. "Young fella like you. Must be something wrong with you upstairs."

After that he avoided Kelly, and the days rolled past without moving him.

In the cafeteria one evening a girl sat next to him. She had the cute monkey-faced look of the prettiest Puerto Ricans—dark eyes and thick hair and a small agile body. She was a room-girl, she said, and she laughed shyly as she told him how the men were always trying to flirt with her, saying "Come in" in the morning and rushing at her in their pajamas.

Duval told her about himself, scarcely believing what he said. "I work in The Beachcomber. I live on the Calle de San Francisco. My wife is going to have a baby." The room-girl was convinced; he was not. This man he was describing, this older employee with the wife: it wasn't him.

The feeling came again, that he was living someone else's life. He was using another man's voice, doing that man's work. And he was surprised by how ordinary the man was, how unambitious: a husband, an employee, and soon to be a father. He listened to himself with curiosity. *I live . . . I work . . . My wife.* The life seemed unshakably simple. How easily the green island had abstracted him and made him this new man.

He continued to work. He could not think what else to do. He had tried to write and had failed. He knew why. Could anything be written in such a cramped room, in such poor light? He fitted his life to the job: the afternoon bus, the phone calls, the chance encounters in the cafeteria, the customers whom he hated and envied, the unvarying drone of the Hawaiian music, the sizzle-splash of frying in the kitchen. Without choosing he had become a different man, and he sometimes wondered whose life he was leading, what name he had.

The money was enough to live on, not enough to free him. So the salary trapped him more completely than the fear of poverty had. The job became central, the only important thing; and his ambitions became local: to take a *público* rather than a bus, to eat in a good restaurant rather than La Gloria, to drink rum instead of beer.

Being away from the room for part of every day abstracted him further, and he always returned on the late bus to find Paula asleep, the Spanish textbook beside her, the light on. Nearly two months had passed since they had come to the island and she was now quite large, with new curves, the full cones of her breasts sloping against her rising belly, the veins showing in her tightened skin. She slept on her side; she walked slowly; she never swam.

She studied Spanish; she didn't learn it. At La Gloria one lunchtime she began timidly to speak. She did so with difficulty, and Duval found himself interrupting, saying a sentence he had not prepared, using words he was unaware he knew and only half understood, *"Lo siento. Yo quiero el mismo, por favor."* The stresses and accents were Puerto Rican, *Joe* for *Yo*, *meemo* for *mismo.*

Whose voice was that?

"Jake!"

He was in bed, being shaken by a damp hand. Paula faced him with tangled hair and her look of worry intensified by the wrinkles of sleep that creased the side of her face.

"Wake up—I'm scared." There was a low roar at the window: the sea, the fury of a distant bus, the wind—he couldn't say.

"What's wrong?"

"I dreamed I had the baby," the sobbed. "It was terrible. You weren't there—oh, God, it hurt. Then they held him up for me to see. Jake, his face was all mangled. It was covered with blood."

Too soon, he thought. This worry shouldn't be mine. But he tried to accept it. He said, "All babies look like that— you've seen pictures of them."

"No—it wasn't the blood," she said, and she grew very quiet, whispering her fearfulness. "It was all deformed. The baby's face was twisted and it was crying. 'It's yours,' they said, 'it's yours.' It was horrible."

He didn't know what to say. But he knew her fear. He saw the infant's bloody distorted face, twisted in accusation. He held Paula and then he was asleep.

In the morning he struggled to wake. The summer heat, 37

the dampness in the air lay motionless against him; pressure, keeping him down. He didn't hear the voices from the street, only the song *"El Pescador,"* with its refrain, *corazón, corazón;* its harsh Puerto Rican sadness. He no longer heard the sea. The sea was drowned by the wind; lost. He had ceased to see the island, its greenness. He had withdrawn to his own island, the room, the woman, the job.

## 4

Paula did not tell him how the Spanish classes reminded her of her old life, the pleasure of uninterrupted study in a clean room, the security of a narrow bed. It was the life she had led before she had met Duval: her girlhood. She wanted it back. She had come to hate the changeless green of the island, the late-summer tinge of yellow exhaustion in the color. She did not tell him how, when he was at work, she never left the room; how she would sleep and wake and think it was another day, and sleep and wake again and imagine that in the space of a few hours she had endured days of seclusion. She had said nothing about the doctor she had seen. The office was dusty, the doctor sweating into his shirt, not noticing his smeared instruments. He smiled (the usual reaction: kindly people tried to share her joy) and after examining her said, "You are—what?—about five months." She was nearly eight. She took all her questions back to the room un-asked.

One hot night she told Duval, "We can give it away."

"What do you mean?" But he was stalling; he knew.

She explained that she had written to a friend in Boston, an old roommate, and the girl had supplied the names of three adoption agencies. Heartbreaking names: one was "The Home for Little Wanderers."

Duval said, "They put them in orphanages."

"No," she said. "They give them to people who can't have children themselves. They're very fussy, too—they check up on the people. They sort of inspect them."

"Then they just hand the kid over."

"Don't pretend to be shocked! You don't want the baby!" She was shouting. In a moment she would cry.

He said, "Do you?"

"I don't want to live like this."

"This is how it would be."

"It could be different," she said. "You could finish college, get your degree—"

"It would always be like this—a room, a job." He could see she was frightened. "We'd quarrel."

"I don't want to fight with you."

He said, "Married people fight."

"Single people fight, too."

"They can walk away."

She said, "That's what you want to do with me—you want to walk away and pretend I don't exist. Admit it! You want to leave me."

"What do you want me to do?"

"I don't know," she said. She had come to dislike her body; she did not recognize it as her own, it was so swollen and unreliable. And she feared the arrival of the baby—feared it most because she knew she would love it and want to keep it, and her life would be over, like that. "Help me," she said. "I feel so ugly."

He said, "You know that doorman, Kelly—the old guy I told you about? I asked him about his job once, and he started to talk about some joint he worked at in Florida. He's got this funny way of talking. He said, 'They wanted me inside once. I was young like you. I said, no sir—I like it out here. Fresh air, meet new people. That's why I'm still here,' he said, 'but I ain't young no more and I don't like it.'"

Paula said, "You're going to leave me."

"I was talking about Kelly."

"We have to decide." She lay on the bed and clasped her stomach as if tenderly enfolding the child. She said, "The poor thing," and then, "No—I don't care what you do, I won't give him away!"

She was insisting he choose, but it seemed to him as if he were past any choice and his life would continue like this, summer after summer, the heat deadening him to the days.

He went to the toilet, which was in darkness. He felt for the light cord and pulled it. For seconds there was stillness, and then the floor moved with cockroaches the heat had enlivened. They ran like large glossy drops and were gone. He had only to wait to see it solved.

40    The next day was Sunday. Paula awoke, and as if the sleep

had been no more than a pause in their conversation she said in an alert accusing voice, "Make up your mind—what are you going to do?"

"We still have a few months."

"Six weeks," she said sharply. "What is it you want?"

He couldn't say, *I want to be a writer*. It seemed as ridiculous as, *I want to be president*. It was partly superstition: saying it might make it untrue. And yet he saw his books, a shelf of them, as clearly as if he had already written them. The conviction had stuck—not that he was to become a writer, but that he had been one secretly for as long as he could remember. To reveal the ambition was to spoil it. And more, to say it was to commit himself to proving it. He wanted someone to verify it in him, to read his face and say, *You are a writer*.

He said, "Do you want to marry me?"

"If we got married we'd be divorced in two years."

He turned away. "Maybe we've had our marriage."

"Is it over so soon? Is that all?" She became angry. "I want more than this."

"So do I!"

"I hate you for hesitating—"

"Hesitating?"

"For bringing me here," she said. "I don't think I could forgive you, even if you did marry me."

He said, "I wish I was forty years old and my life was behind me."

"That shows how young you are," she said, almost exulting. "Men of forty aren't old! You don't know anything." 41

Later, walking down the Calle de San Francisco to lunch at La Gloria, she said, "In six weeks there are going to be three of us. Think about that and you won't feel so smart."

But having said it she grew sad and couldn't eat, and after lunch she said it was too hot for the beach.

Duval went back to the room with her and dressed for work. It was only two o'clock; he was not due at the restaurant until five. He left her on the bed with her Spanish book, in the posture that put her to sleep. A bus in the plaza bore the destination sign LOIZA. He boarded the bus and rode to the end of the line.

Loiza was not as he had imagined, a shady corner at the forest's edge, a frontier. It was simply a leaning signpost where the bus stopped and turned around. The street, wide and useless, continued through a drab suburb of stucco bungalows. There were some palms along the roadside, but they were not green, and dead fronds like the ruined plumage of an enormous bird lay in the broken street. Political slogans with their enclosing exclamation marks were painted on the bungalow walls and on some lampposts were pictures of the president, Muñoz Marin. No sun, only a low cloud as gray as metal radiated humid heat. Duval walked down the sidewalk and saw more of the Sunday emptiness, cracked bungalows, grass growing through blisters in the asphalt, and from behind the dusty hedges the radio's tin rhumba, "*El Pescador*" and *corazón*.

He walked to a road junction and ahead saw a parking lot filled with cars, and above a sign, CANTO GALLO. He welcomed the noise and hurried toward it.

It was a *galleria*, a cockpit. He bought a ticket for the middle tier, but as he started through the door he faced confusion—men counting money, men running down the passage, gamblers quarreling—and to avoid them he slipped through a side door and down a short flight of stairs.

The room smelled of straw and chicken droppings and was stacked with wooden cages holding small skinny roosters. They scratched and squawked, but there was in their crowing something still of the farmyard, the shady unfenced Puerto Rican plot with its standpipe and sprinklings of corn. They fussed, yet looked calm, and Duval found it odd to see them in these vertical piles, crammed in such a small space.

He wandered around the room, looking closely at the birds, noticing their bright eyes, the shine of their feathers, the wrinkled bunch of scrotumlike tissue draped on their heads, their oversized feet and stained claws. He heard Paula speaking, saw her face, and in her face a demand. *Choose, choose*, she was saying.

But each time he framed a reply, a shout went up from behind the wall of this fowlcoop, in the cockpit—triumphant cries of yelling laughter. The cries became more frequent and lost the laughter, and they were accompanied by a stamping of many feet which shook the beams over his head. The howling sounded neither Spanish nor English; it was no language; it was encouragement, anger, jeering, the noise of people watching a small hero, an insignificant victim; a mob's praise.

The crouching roosters on their shelves of cages seemed to hear it. They stuck their heads through the wooden bars and 43 jerked their necks, so their jeweled staring eyes turned in wonderment. Duval paced the room. The cocks pecked hard at their padlocks. *It's up to you*, she was saying.

He was about to go away—to leave the *galleria* entirely— when three men entered the small room. They were excited, jabbering in Spanish, arguing without facing each other. One stayed at the door glowering at Duval. The other two went to the stack of cages and took out two cocks, a black one, a brown one, and quickly trussed them with lengths of cord. The birds fought and flapped while their legs were tied, then lay still, two parcels of feathers, like a pair of brushes. The men were attaching spurs to the birds' legs when the man at the door spoke.

"Go," he said crossly to Duval and gestured for him to leave.

Duval went upstairs and took a seat in the middle tier. Most of the seats were empty, but near him, in the section that surrounded the circle of the pit, the seats were full, and it was only there, up front, that he saw women, two or three. It was like the interior of a primitive circus. The roof seemed propped on shafts of dusty sunlight; and the rough unpainted wood and the dust rising from the shallow pit and its suffo-cating smallness lent it an unmistakable air of cruelty.

Brass scales were brought out, the chains and pans jan-gling, and the trussed cocks were placed in the pans and bal-anced. The two pairs of bound feet hovered at the same level. The scales were raised for the audience to see. There was chattering throughout the ritual of weighing, but as the 44 scales were removed the gallery became frenzied—men called across the pit, shouting numbers and waving dollar bills. One man vaulted the low fence and hurried across the pit to shake a wad of money in another's frowning face.

The birds were untied, but instead of releasing them the owners faced each other, holding them forward and slowly circling, keeping the beaks a few inches apart, struggling against the flapping wings and angry reaching beaks. The cocks' eyes were blazing as the men solemnly set them down.

Now Duval saw the spurs, inch-long claws clamped to their legs, which gave them a fierce strutting look. The black one began to run around the margin of the pit.

The squawks were drowned by the shouts from the audience, and the birds flew at each other. They did not appear to use the spurs. They fluttered a foot from the ground, seeming to balance on their downthrust wings, and they threw their heads forward and bore down, snatching and pecking with their beaks. The brown one rose higher, pecked harder and pinioned the black one clumsily with clawing feet. He beat him down with his wings and drove his beak into the black one's head. They tumbled in the dust, crazily magnetized, and then chased each other in circles around the pit, with outstretched necks, moving gracefully flat-footed, driving dust and feathers into the air.

*No*, thought Duval, and he was deafened by the cries from the audience. The brown cock flew and settled against the black one, plucking the reddened head.

The black one had started to weaken. One wing was askew, and it scraped the ground with it and tottered on it as it toiled away from the other. The brown one screamed and 45 beat its wings and attacked again. The wing flaps, the flutter of feathers simulating the opening of a Chinese fan, sounded harmless, but it masked the damage. When they were close Duval could see how the cocks' heads were both swollen and their feathers ragged. The audience was excited, beginning to stamp the supporting planks of the gallery and shake the wooden benches.

Like old hindering skirts, the wings of the black cock hung down, and he wobbled in panic around the pit, the brown one behind him, leaping and pecking. The black one fell and crooked his feet against the brown one's attack, and finally, in a helpless effort to fight back, offered his bleeding head to the other's furious beak.

There were cheers; the owners stepped in; the cheering stopped. The audience showed no further interest in the birds. Money was changing hands and men had gathered in groups to argue about the result.

Duval followed the owners back to the fowlcoop. The cocks were placed on a table and examined. The brown one which had been so lively was feebly twitching its legs as its owner ran his fingers through the tufts of feathers to search for wounds. The black one lay as if dead; the scrotal comb was torn and its head was split all over and leaking blood. The owner prodded it gently and murmured in Spanish. Then he lifted its damaged eyelids and said sadly, *"Mira."* He showed the empty eye sockets of the blinded bird.

*No,* thought Duval again, and back in the street, walking
 to the bus stop through the suburb that now had a look of

pure horror, his reflection came to him whole: *I will never get married.*

5

The sun, glimmering and enlarged by cloud, was at the level of the treetops, balanced on the upper thickness of palm fronds, as Duval walked to work. The opposite side of the street was marked by the sunset's pickets of shadow, flung from the palm trunks, and in this broken light women strolled, some singly, some in pairs.

Mr. Boder was in front of the restaurant talking to Kelly. What struck Duval at once was that Mr. Boder was crowding the old man as he spoke and peering into his face, almost bumping him with his nose. When Duval spoke Mr. Boder stepped back.

"Looking at the action," said Mr. Boder, with the kind of disguising heartiness he used on customers. He nodded at the women.

Kelly looked crestfallen. He said nothing.

"Professionals," said Duval. He winked at Kelly. *"Por la noche."*

"I'd like to jump all over that one," said Mr. Boder. He licked his lips. "I'm overdue for a strange piece."

It was a vicious phrase. Duval saw him taste it. The women wore tight dresses with a slash to show their legs, and 47 they walked with a slow rolling movement and swung large handbags. But it was the shoes that gave them away. The spike heels were worn down from their continual pacing, giving them an unsteadiness that made them lurch tipsily every few steps.

Duval said, "That one's smiling. I think she likes you."

Mr. Boder's face tightened, as if he had been mocked. He said, "Come inside. I want to know why you're late." And without another word he entered the restaurant.

Kelly said, "Oh, me."

"What's wrong?"

"I just got me walking papers."

"He fired you?" Duval was puzzled. "What for?"

"They owes me money. I axed him for it. He told me I was sassing him." But Kelly was smiling. "I'se a doorman without no door."

"You're joking."

"Boy," said Kelly. "You better go on in there or you're going to be out on your ear, too."

Duval went inside and put on his Beachcomber blazer. In the foyer of the restaurant he saw Mr. Boder seated at the telephone.

Mr. Boder said, "I've been doing your work for you. Look at these reservations." He showed Duval the diary with the column of names in his oversize handwriting. "Now, where the hell have you been?"

"Waiting for a bus." He would not say he had been to a cockfight. The sight had terrified him and he could not repeat what he had seen: the bright jeweled eye plucked out, the scrap of white tissue in the eye socket, the dripping blinded head of the bird.

"If you're late again I'll dock your salary—your wife won't like that, will she?" Mr. Boder stood up. "What did that crazy old man tell you out front?"

Duval said angrily, "Did you fire him?"

Mr. Boder did not reply immediately. He walked toward the bar and then, as if remembering, turned and said loudly, "You mind your own business, sonny, if you know what's good for you."

Duval picked up the diary. It was the Cuban's night off; Sundays were quiet. A dozen customers came and went, and the waiters were impatient, drumming their fingers on their trays, complaining in murmurs, and watching for the front door to open.

Duval went outside. Kelly was gone.

The next night there was a Puerto Rican at the door. It was only when Duval saw the baggy wrinkled uniform on the man that he realized how tall Kelly had been. Duval avoided speaking to Mr. Boder that night, and at closing time, he was indignant and sad. He wanted a drink. It was a hotel rule that employees off duty were to leave the premises. The casino, the coffee shop, the pool, the bars were closed to him; and he knew he could be fired for breaking that rule.

Duval went to the hotel's veranda bar, where the drinks were slightly cheaper than inside, and sat and had three shots of rum. He drank them straight, in the Puerto Rican way, finishing with a glass of water. Then he stumbled down the gravel driveway to the bus stop. No one had seen him.

A woman came toward him from behind a palm, her heels clicking on the sidewalk, the revealing wobble in her step. Her hair was drawn back tightly and even in the street lamp's poor light he could see that her dress was soiled. She was short and had a small mouth stamped in her sharp face.

She said, "Want a date, mister?"

"How much?"

"Ten dollars."

Duval went through his pockets. He found a dollar and some change. He had spent the rest of his tips at the bar. He said, "I'm nineteen—don't I get a discount?"

She recognized the word and laughed. "Even the young ones, they pay me."

"I don't have any money."

*"Nada por nada,"* she said. *"Buenos noches, chico."*

"Wait," said Duval. "Where are you from—San Juan?"

"Habana."

"You like San Juan?"

"I like this." She touched her thighs and jerked her hips at him. She leered: gold teeth.

That aroused him, and though it was after midnight when he got back to the old part of the city he went to La Gloria. It was closed; a man was stacking chairs on the bar. In the plaza he could see the homeless boys sleeping curled up on the stone benches, small still corpses on the slabs. He walked up the Calle de San Francisco. The street was empty, but he kept walking, looking in doorways. He turned into a narrow cobblestone street and headed down the hill, past darkened 50 shops and small hotels, feeling the rum's warmth still in his throat and a fatigue from work that gave him a nervous inaccurate strength and a quick stride.

He barely heard the woman's greeting. She had been seated on a bench; she rose and said hello as he passed. The sound reached him. She was asking for a cigarette.

He offered her one and lit it, and in the match flare he saw her lined face, the dress a bit too big, the firelit strand of black hair loose at her eyes. She looked cautious, almost afraid.

He said, "What's your name?"

"Anna," she said, and glanced down the street. "You want to go with me?"

"Yes," he said.

"Five dollars."

"I don't have five dollars."

"Four dollars," she said. "Let we go."

He fished in his pockets, knowing what he would bring out. He showed her the dollar, he rattled the change.

She said, "You don't respect me."

"Please," he said.

"No." She walked away. He followed her down the sidewalk, and when she stopped before a storefront he was encouraged.

"Anna," he said softly.

"You see?" She was tapping the plate glass of the shop window.

He saw a rack of shoes and looked away. They were tiny; children's shoes, small laced things with price tags, mounted on stands.

51

"Look," she said, urging him. "These things cost money."

It was too late; he had seen the pathetic shoes and the prices, and all his desire died.

He entered the room, but did not switch on the light. He undressed in the darkness and slipped beneath the sheet. Paula rolled toward him. She took his head and drew it to her, and he could hear the slow thump of her heart against her breast. He nestled against her, hating the thought that he had betrayed her and was, embracing and kissing her, betraying her still.

Paula awoke in tears, and he felt a helpless sorrow for her as she sobbed. The child, her stomach, shook.

"It's not fair to me," she said. "It's not fair to him. The poor baby."

He knew what to say, but not how to say it. She was so easily frightened.

She said, "We don't have much time."

Choose, she was saying. But he had chosen long ago; he had discovered his small green soul on the island, its solitary inward conceit scribbled differently from hers, and now he could read the scribble.

"Poor Kelly," he said. He saw him, the clown, the limp mustache, the green frock coat and braided cap. The old man moped toward him, chattering, blinded, indicating his flat shoes with a crooked finger: *Them's my Hoover shoes.*

Paula said, "I'm not staying here much longer—I'm not having my baby on this miserable island. I'm going to catch a plane while they'll still let me. Women can't fly if they're more than eight months pregnant." She looked at him strangely. "You didn't even know that."

"What about the tickets?"

"I've been to the bank. We've got the airfare now—enough for two tickets home."

"After that?"

"It's up to you."

" 'My baby'—that's what you said."

She cried again, hearing her own words repeated. "I don't want him," she said, her mouth curling sorrowfully. "I want to go back to school and do well. I want to marry someone who loves me. I want a nice house."

Duval thought: *I don't want any of those things;* but he wouldn't upset her by saying what he did want.

She said, "And I don't want to be a failure."

"You won't fail."

"What do you know?" she said. "What do you do after you give a child away?"

"You start again," he said. "Alone."

"You have no more chances. If you fail then, you have nothing."

"No," he said, but he only said it to oppose her, to offer encouragement.

"Nothing at all," she said bitterly. *"Nada."*

"It's a gamble," he said.

"It's a human sacrifice."

* * *

He was deliberately late for work that day, but instead of confronting him Mr. Boder ignored him. Duval heard him shouting in the kitchen.

The Cuban was listening, too. He said, "I hate that pig."

"Then why do you put up with him?"

"This isn't my country," he said. "They could throw me out." He kicked gloomily at the carpet. "I got a wife and two *niños*."

Mr. Boder came out of the kitchen. "What's up—nothing to do? Who's watching that phone?"

The Cuban said, "I am."

"Come here, Castro. I've got a job for you." Mr. Boder went close to Duval and peered at him. He said, "Keep it up. You're asking for it."

Duval stared at him. He had said that to Kelly.

"Move that chair. Someone's going to trip over it."

"It's not in the way."

"Are you deaf?"

Duval moved the chair, and in this tiny act of obedience he saw humiliating surrender. But his timidity was for hire: he was to blame.

"He's worried," said the Cuban later. "The vice chancellor of the university is coming from Rio Piedras with his whole family. He wants to make a good figure."

It was true. At nine-thirty the man came. He was a thin dapper man with a narrow head and a mustache fringing his upper lip. He held his young son's hand, and his wife followed, shepherding two older girls in white dresses.

But there was a further surprise. At ten the Beachcomber

arrived. It was wholly unexpected and Duval could see the shock on Mr. Boder's face when the door swung open and the Beachcomber dragged his wooden leg through and tapped his way forward, rocking on the leg, balancing with the cane. The Puerto Rican waiters barely recognized him, and watched the way he moved with the contempt they offered all cripples.

"Boder!" said the Beachcomber before Mr. Boder could speak.

"This is a pleasant surprise," said Mr. Boder, regaining himself, grinning, hesitating in a bow.

"I was in Santo Domingo," said the Beachcomber. His hair was slightly longer, but he wore the same short-sleeved Hawaiian shirt that showed his tattoos.

"Fascinating place," said Mr. Boder.

"They shot Trujillo this afternoon," said the Beachcomber. "I took the first plane and got the hell out. Why is this place so goddamned empty?"

"Slow night," said Mr. Boder. "Very unusual. Right this way."

The Beachcomber paused and shifted his weight from his good leg to the cane. He said, "Looks like Thursday at the city morgue."

Mr. Boder, smiling, did not appear to hear. He fussed with the reservations diary and then started to speak.

"Get me a drink," said the Beachcomber and moved off heavily, in the direction of the dining room.

"Right you are," said Mr. Boder, still grinning, showing his yellow capped teeth at the Beachcomber's back.

The waiters had gathered in a little group by one of the carved Polynesian statues. They were whispering. Duval heard *Trujillo* and *muerte*.

Mr. Boder brought a tall glass to where the Beachcomber was sitting. He sat sloppily, his wooden leg propped on a chair, scratching his tattoos, and squinting crossly at the nearly empty dining room. Duval saw him as a fraud, a tycoon in old clothes, a figure of crass romance. The Beachcomber was staring at the vice chancellor, who was deep in conversation with a waiter. They were talking about Trujillo. Another waiter came over to confirm it. Duval heard *verdad*. In minutes the whole restaurant knew what the Beachcomber had only muttered.

"Very unusual," Mr. Boder was saying, bowing as he spoke.

Duval was behind him.

Mr. Boder turned and hissed, "Where's Castro?"

"I don't like it," the Beachcomber was saying. "You can do better than this, Boder."

"Eating," said Duval.

"Get him," said Mr. Boder. "And make it snappy. While you're at it get another cloth for the table—this one's filthy. Oh, and don't think"—Mr. Boder was still hissing, but he was also smiling, half-turned to the Beachcomber—"don't think I didn't notice you were late for work. I've got something to say to you later. Now move."

"Boder—" Duval heard the Beachcomber say as he left
56  the dining room.

He went through the kitchen to the hotel cafeteria. The waiters had brought the news here of Trujillo's assassination and there were groups of Puerto Ricans in the corridor talking excitedly. An elderly Negro moved among them slapping his mop on the tiles.

Duval was lost in thought. *Your wife wouldn't like that.* He tried to swallow his anger. Five minutes had passed; ten before he got to the cafeteria. He paused at the door, hating the noise, the plates banging, the voices. They were talking about Trujillo. Already the repetition of this news irritated Duval. He saw the Cuban, eating alone, forking food to his mouth.

Twenty minutes: nothing. But it was too long. In that small delay was his refusal. He winced, thinking of Mr. Boder's anger. He could never again return to the restaurant. He was finished here, as lightly as he had begun.

It was—this hesitation—as much of a choice as he needed to make. And he had hung up his blazer and was walking past the floodlit palms of the hotel driveway before he realized the enormity of what he had done. Then Mr. Boder, the Beachcomber, the waiters, everyone there seemed suddenly very small, no larger than children; and children had no memory.

It was so simple to go. Now he knew how. You walked away without a sound and kept walking. Beyond the lush hotel garden he saw light, but it was the moon behind the trees that lit them so strangely, darkening the green, like smoke beginning.

He decided to walk the mile home. As he walked on the

sea road to the old part of the city the moon rose, seeming to wet the palms with its light. The wind was on the sea, and the waves tumbled like lost cargoes of silver smashing to pieces on the beach.